Katie Woo

No More Teasing

by Fran Manushkin

illustrated by Tammie Lyon

Picture Window Books
Minneapolis, Minnesota

Katie Woo is published by Picture Window Books
A Capstone Imprint
1710 Roe Crest Drive
North Mankato, MN 56003
www.capstonepub.com

Text © 2010 Fran Manushkin
Illustrations © 2010 Picture Window Books

Library of Congress Cataloging-in-Publication Data
Manushkin, Fran.
    No more teasing / by Fran Manushkin; illustrated by Tammie Lyon.
    p. cm. — (Katie Woo)
    ISBN 978-1-4048-5492-5 (library binding)
    ISBN 978-1-4048-6056-8 (softcover)
    [1. Bullies—Fiction. 2. Teasing—Fiction. 3. Schools—Fiction.
4. Chinese Americans—Fiction.] I. Lyon, Tammie, ill. II. Title.
PZ7.M3195No 2010
[E]—dc22   2009002190

Summary: The class bully loves to tease Katie Woo until she decides to ignore him.

Creative Director: Heather Kindseth
Graphic Designer: Emily Harris

Photo Credits
Fran Manushkin, pg. 26
Tammie Lyon, pg. 26

Printed in the United States of America in Stevens Point, Wisconsin.
052012
006770R

 Table of Contents

Chapter 1
Mean Roddy

One day, on the way to

school, Katie Woo tripped.

She fell into the mud. Splat!

She scraped her knee, and

mud got on her new sweater

and all of her books.

Katie started

to cry.

"Cry baby! Cry baby!"

yelled Roddy Rogers.

Katie's feelings were so

hurt, she cried harder.

Roddy grinned.

At school, Roddy Rogers

kept teasing Katie during

recess.

"Go away!" she told him.

But Roddy didn't.

At lunch,

they had pizza,

Katie's favorite.

She took such a big bite

that she got tomato sauce on

her nose and cheeks.

"Look at Katie," Roddy shouted. "Katie's got a goopy face!"

Roddy said, "Goopy face! Goopy face!"

"Stop it!" cried Katie. But Roddy didn't stop. He was having too much fun.

Roddy made
faces at Katie all
day long.

When Katie stuck
her tongue out at him, he
made more faces. Ugly ones.

"How can I make Roddy

stop teasing me?" Katie

asked her friend JoJo.

But JoJo didn't know.

Chapter 2
The Amazing Butterfly

The next day, Roddy

teased Katie when she was

running at recess. And he

teased her when she was

trying to read her book.

Katie was so unhappy. She
didn't want to go to school
anymore.

The next day, Miss Winkle told the class, "Everyone, our butterflies are ready to hatch. Please hurry over and watch them!"

Katie pushed up her glasses.

"Hey, I see four eyes!"

Roddy said in a quiet voice.

He knew if Miss Winkle heard

him, he would get in trouble.

Katie was about to

say something back. But

suddenly, her butterfly began

hatching.

It was so amazing. She

couldn't take her eyes off it!

Roddy said, "Four eyes!" a little louder.

But Katie kept watching her butterfly.

Roddy was so mad. He slammed his desk and hurt his finger.

Chapter 3
Stop Teasing!

Later, the class worked

on their "Good Neighbors"

paintings with a partner.

Roddy snuck over to Katie

and said, "Ew! Your painting

is ugly!"

But Katie loved painting so
much that she kept doing it.

"Hey!" Roddy said. "Didn't
you hear me?"

Katie still didn't answer.

Roddy got so mad that he smeared black paint all over his part of his picture.

"Hey!" his partner yelled. "You ruined our painting!"

On the way home, Roddy

glared at Katie, but she

didn't even look at him.

Katie began smiling

and smiling.

When JoJo sat down,

Katie told her, "I'm so happy!

I know how to make Roddy

stop teasing me."

"What do you do?"

asked JoJo.

"Nothing!" Katie said. "When I don't cry or yell, Roddy isn't having fun, so he stops teasing me."

"Katie Woo, you are one smart girl," said JoJo.

"Thanks!" said Katie. And she smiled all the way home.

About the Author

Fran Manushkin is the author of many popular picture books, including *How Mama Brought the Spring; Baby, Come Out!; Latkes and Applesauce: A Hanukkah Story;* and *The Tushy Book.* There is a real Katie Woo — she's Fran's great-niece — but she never gets in half the trouble of the Katie Woo in the books. Fran writes on her beloved Mac computer in New York City, without the help of her two naughty cats, Cookie and Goldy.

About the Illustrator

Tammie Lyon began her love for drawing at a young age while sitting at the kitchen table with her dad. She continued her love of art and eventually attended the Columbus College of Art and Design, where she earned a bachelors degree in fine art. After a brief career as a professional ballet dancer, she decided to devote herself full time to illustration. Today she lives with her husband, Lee, in Cincinnati, Ohio. Her dogs, Gus and Dudley, keep her company as she works in her studio.

 Glossary

amazing (ah-MAZE-ing)—causing sudden surprise or wonder

favorite (FAY-vuh-rit)—the thing that is liked best

goopy (GOO-pee)—messy or sticky

hatching (HACH-ing)—breaking out of an egg or cocoon

ruined (ROO-ind)—spoiled or destroyed something

smeared (SMEERD)—rubbed something over a surface, making it messy

🌸 Discussion Questions 🌸

1. Katie was so sad when she fell in the mud. What could you have said to make her feel better?

2. What do you think Miss Winkle would have done if she heard Roddy calling Katie names?

3. Katie figured out a great way to get Roddy to stop teasing her. Are there other ways she could have gotten him to stop?

Writing Prompts

1. Roddy was not being a good classmate. Write down three rules that could help him be a better classmate.

2. The children were painting "Good Neighbors" pictures. What sort of things could go in this type of painting? Write a list.

3. Roddy is a bully. Write down five words that describe a bully.

Having Fun with Katie Woo

In *No More Teasing*, Katie Woo's class is working on "Good Neighbors" paintings. It is fun to make a piece of art with other people. Try making a picture with a partner and practice working together.

What you need:

- a large piece of poster board. It should be big enough that both of you can gather around it.
- art supplies like pencils, markers, crayons, paints, etc.

Getting started

1. Decide what your picture's theme will be. You should both agree on a theme together.

2. Divide the poster into sections. Each of you will get your own area to work on. You might also want to save a section for words that describe your theme. For example, "Our favorite animals" describes a pet theme.

3. Before you start drawing, talk to your partner about what you will each draw. You might also want to talk about what colors you will use. That way your sections will look nice together.

4. Now start drawing and painting! Before you know it, your teamwork will result in a beautiful picture.